GRANDPA PUTTER AND GRANNY HOE

YEARLING BOOKS are designed especially to entertain and enlighten young people. Patricia Reilly Giff, consultant to this series, received her bachelor's degree from Marymount College and a master's degree in history from St. John's University. She holds a Professional Diploma in Reading and a Doctorate of Humane Letters from Hofstra University. She was a teacher and reading consultant for many years, and is the author of numerous books for young readers.

For a complete listing of all Yearling titles, write to
Dell Readers Service,
P.O. Box 1045,
South Holland, IL 60473.

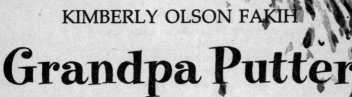

KIMBERLY OLSON FAKIH

Grandpa Putter and Granny Hoe

Pictures by
TRACEY CAMPBELL PEARSON

A Yearling Book

Published by
Bantam Doubleday Dell Books for Young Readers
a division of
Bantam Doubleday Dell Publishing Group, Inc.
1540 Broadway
New York, New York 10036

ISBN: 0-440-41078-9

Reprinted by arrangement with Farrar Straus Giroux

Printed in the United States of America

April 1996

10 9 8 7 6 5 4 3 2 1

CWO

*Dedicated to a place called Bemidji, Minnesota,
our nation's cold spot.*
—KOF

*For Greg and Catherine's
Grandma and Bopa*
—TCP

Contents

GRANDPA PUTTER AND GRANNY HOE

Celebrating

Neep! Neep! Grandpa Putter honked his horn and waited for Jazz and Koo in the driveway. His car was long and white as a ship. The front of it looked like a wide-eyed face with a toothy smile. Inside, it was as shiny-bright and clean as Grandpa's white patent-leather shoes.

Grandpa usually had a driver to take him places. But today he drove himself. He watched from behind the wheel as Jazz and Koo came toward him.

"Ready or not!" he called to Koo, who had been ready for weeks. Koo had packed and unpacked his suitcase three times, and had almost forgotten to take his clown night-light from his room.

"Time to go!" Grandpa shouted to Jazz, who had looked at her watch all morning, waiting till it would be Time to Go. She had packed her suitcase once, and had tucked *her* clown night-light into the bag before anything else.

"Coming, Grandpa!" Koo shrieked. He nearly fell over himself trying to be first to the car.

"Hello, Grandpa," Jazz said calmly. She was three minutes older than Koo, and she did not care about baby things like being first.

Grandpa Putter got out of the car and helped them put their bags in the back seat. Koo hurled himself into the front seat, followed by Jazz. Before Grandpa closed the door, he pushed his hat back from his brow with his duck-head cane. "Happy birthday, scamps. Did you tell your parents goodbye?" he asked. He tried to smooth the blue-and-white stripes of his tidy suit.

"Seven times," answered Koo, who was swinging the two pairs of tiny metal shoes attached to the dashboard. They looked as if they had been dipped in gold. A few years ago,

Celebrating

those shoes had belonged to Jazz and Koo. Grandpa nodded and slammed the door shut. He eased into the driver's seat and started the car.

"We told them goodbye so many times," added Jazz, thinking that Koo's answer hadn't been very interesting, "that they said they couldn't finish packing until we left."

"They're going across the ocean," Koo said. It was the first trip their parents had taken without them.

"To Europe," Jazz said. Their mother designed children's sports clothes, and their father sold them. They would be gone for weeks.

"That's right," Grandpa said. "And now we're off!"

Koo sat forward, watching everything Grandpa did. Ready or Not. Jazz settled into the seat, her eyes closed. Time to Go.

The tires squealed as Grandpa Putter backed out of the driveway. They were on their way.

The tires squeaked as he jerked the car to a stop. They were not on their way, after all.

"Tarnation!" he said, getting out of the car. Jazz and Koo turned around in their seats to see where he was going. A familiar truck, dirty as farmer's boots, was parked behind them and blocked their path.

"Halloo, my dears," Granny Hoe called from the truck's front seat. Two American flags fluttered on either side of the fenders. A rabbit's foot dangled from the rearview mirror. In the back, bushel baskets and gardening tools were flung around like bits of Koo's puzzles, which Jazz always had to help put together.

"Hello, Mr. Putter," Granny said to Grandpa. She poked one hand out the window for a handshake. Grandpa Putter waved her off. Jazz and Koo got out of the car to watch.

"You're in the way!" he sputtered. "We're going to the toy store and then to my club for Jazz and Koo's birthday lunch and *we're* late!"

"I'm just in time," Granny Hoe said, getting out of the truck. "I closed the store. I bought ice cream on the way over. I made pineapple cookies with cherry frosting for the children. I want them to have their birthday party at my house."

"We've been all through this," Grandpa Putter stormed. "They're staying at my house during the week, because it's closer to school. You get them on weekends. But their parents

Celebrating

said that for special times, the schedule could change. Today *is* special—their birthday is all planned." His face was red above his bright white shirt collar. Jazz and Koo knew this was the first sign that he was mad.

"We're late!" Grandpa said again, grabbing the gold watch in his vest pocket and looking at it. That was the second sign. He was getting really angry.

Jazz and Koo moved closer to each other.

"Let's not spoil such a beautiful day for a party," Granny Hoe answered smoothly. "Come on, children, you can ride in the back of the truck, if you hold on. And I'll show you who is living in the birdhouse I made for you."

Grandpa yanked his watch chain. A vest button sailed through the air, landed on the driveway, and rolled away into the grass. His face was now purple.

Jazz looked at Koo.

They loved the toy store and lunch at the club. "Ten desserts to choose from," Jazz whispered to Koo.

Koo looked at Jazz.

They loved riding in the truck and wanted

Celebrating

to see the birdhouse. "Pineapple cookies with cherry frosting," Koo whispered back.

"We'll go shopping now with Grandpa," Jazz said in a loud voice, taking Koo's hand.

"Have lunch at the club," Koo added, slipping his other hand into Granny Hoe's.

"And then Grandpa will drop us off at Granny's for the party!" Jazz finished, tugging at Grandpa Putter's hand with her free one.

"Well! It *means* we'll have to rush," Grandpa Putter said, picking up his vest button.

"The ice cream will *melt*," Granny Hoe added, getting into her truck.

"It will have to do," Grandpa Putter grumbled.

"Yes, yes, I suppose it will," Granny Hoe groaned.

Making Signs

In the back of Granny Hoe's hardware store was a heavy pine desk where she paid her bills, counted her money, and kept her records. The following Saturday, Jazz and Koo sat on either side of the desk, making signs for Granny to hang by the cash register at the front of the store.

Signs they had made in the past were already up front: NAME YOUR ITEM, STEP RIGHT IN, THIS WAY TO ALL YOUR ROOFING NEEDS, WATCH YOUR STEP, and five others, NO TELEPHONE, DEFINITELY NO CREDIT CARDS, NO SOLICITORS, NO

Making Signs

TWO-PARTY CHECKS, and NO CAT LITTER. A yellowed photograph of Granny Hoe's husband was taped up next to the signs. Jazz and Koo knew good stories about him because Granny and her customers talked about him sometimes. But he had not been around for many years, not since they were babies.

Granny printed the words for the signs on scraps of paper. Jazz and Koo first copied each letter with a pencil onto a piece of large tan cardboard. Then they painted the letters and decorated around them. Granny Hoe made both children wear long aprons all spattered with paint like colored stars. The aprons covered their clothes from collars to shoes.

"My sign has flowers," Koo said. SEED SALE was printed with crooked letters. Koo always painted better flowers than Jazz. He knew it. So did she.

"When people see those blossoms, they'll buy more seeds," Granny Hoe told him. "I'm lucky you know how to decorate the signs for me."

Jazz tugged Granny Hoe's sweater. Her sign said NO CHECKS. Her letters were straight as soldiers in smart new uniforms. Jazz always printed better than Koo. She knew it. So did he.

It bothered her that she couldn't make flowers, so she had added wavy green lines. "It's ivy," she told Granny Hoe.

Granny Hoe was sorting nails, nuts, and bolts into small drawers and old cigar boxes. She glanced up. "It's lovely," she said to Jazz. "Like the wall ivy I have at home."

"Next time," said Jazz, "I want to make up my own signs."

"We can spell now, Granny Hoe," Koo declared.

"One of us can spell now," Jazz reminded him. "You need a sign that says your store is best," she told Granny.

"My customers already know that," Granny answered. "A sign won't help."

"But what about people who don't know?" Koo asked.

"Maybe you'll tell them for me," Granny Hoe replied.

The bell over the door jingled. A customer!

"I'll get it," Jazz called, starting toward the front of the store.

"No, I'll get it," Koo cried, following her.

To go to the front of the store they had to walk around all the clutter of items Granny Hoe stuffed into every nook and corner, like a tangled forest. And they had to be careful not to knock anything down.

"I'll be first," Koo yelled after Jazz. "I'm going to fly over."

Jazz ignored him. She ducked under the mixing machine which stirred the paint from two different cans into one smooth color. She placed her small foot inside each of the large painted footprints that traced the way to the rack of hammers, saws, screwdrivers, and pliers, before they veered off toward the front door.

"I'm almost there!" Koo called. He ran past the side door that led to the junkyard, full of bent wheels, rusty parts, barrels of new parts in oil, and rotting lumber.

Jazz moved down the china aisle and saw the two angels whose wings changed color whenever it rained. Afraid the wobbly stacks of dishes would tip, she headed toward items that were not breakable: cookie cutters, plastic measuring cups, pie plates, baking tins, loaf pans, and wooden spoons.

Making Signs

Koo dashed by a giant spool of ropes, chains, hosing, and wire. He could hear Jazz—she wasn't even hurrying. He turned left at the glass animals by the side door. To keep his distance from the shelves, he ran his finger along the row of light bulbs screwed into a board. Doorknobs were fastened to tiny doors on the wall. Next to them was a stack of mailboxes, in dull gray metal with bright red flags. Copper pans and brand-new brooms stood in one corner. When he smiled into a copper pan, his face looked funny—not round and smooth, but long and bony. Above the pan, a row of clown night-lights grinned down at him.

Up ahead Koo spotted Jazz turning the last corner.

"I win," he called, but it was only half-hearted—he knew he was too late.

The front of the store smelled like dust and wood and new paint. Jars of jam and preserves made from Granny's garden were on shelves by the cash register. Jazz saw the back of the customer bent over a display of keys. Rows and rows of them hung on a rack like jewels.

Sometimes Granny Hoe let Jazz and Koo string the keys like beads.

"Can I help you?" Jazz asked, just the way she had heard Granny say it.

"I should hope so," Grandpa Putter said, turning around. Jazz hugged him. "I need some lawn seed."

"Hello, Grandpa," Koo said, tugging at Grandpa's jacket.

Granny Hoe peeked through the shelves. "What can I get you, Mr. Putter?" she asked.

"Lawn seed," Grandpa Putter told her. "I'm having some men seed my lawn."

"Lawn seed is on sale," said Koo. He pointed to the sign in Granny's hands: SEED SALE.

"Wonderful," Grandpa Putter answered. "I'll take two bags."

"It's not on sale until the sign is up," Granny Hoe told him. "Full price till then."

Grandpa Putter frowned. He looked at Jazz and Koo. Jazz didn't know what to say. "Okay, I'll take it," Grandpa said. He pulled out his checkbook.

"No checks," Granny Hoe told him. She held up Jazz's sign for him.

Making Signs

"Not until the sign is up," Grandpa Putter replied.

Granny Hoe frowned. She looked at Jazz and Koo. Koo didn't know what to say. "Okay," Granny said, "I'll take it."

Dressing Up

Most days at Grandpa Putter's were exactly the same.

Every morning when Jazz and Koo woke up, Grandpa's housekeeper, Rosalind, brought them toast and honey and two kinds of juice for breakfast. Ben, Grandpa's driver, took them to school, and he picked them up at three o'clock. Every afternoon, they went riding at Grandpa's stables on a pony named Cowdy. Each evening, Rosalind filled the tub with bubbles twice.

Sometimes Jazz went first.

Other times Koo went first.

But no matter who went first, there were

always fluffy towels to dry them and powder that made them smell good.

And every night after their baths, Grandpa took them Out for Dinner, dressed up in their best clothes.

Since it was almost summer, Jazz and Koo flew their kites after dinner in Grandpa's back yard. If it rained, they played games in the library, by the fireplace. Grandpa usually told them stories about when he was their age, until he fell asleep.

While he dozed in his brown leather chair, Jazz and Koo pulled out his collection of marble soldiers from the liquor and tobacco cabinet. They marched them over the furniture and up and down the hallways until it was time to go to bed. If Grandpa didn't tuck them in, Rosalind did.

"I look nice!" Koo exclaimed one night. He stood in front of his bedroom mirror at Grandpa's admiring his new suit jacket and tie. Jazz bounced on his bed.

"I look like Grandpa!" he said. He puffed on a pencil, the way Grandpa smoked a cigar, with one hand behind his back. Koo rocked on his feet. Back and forth. Then he noticed his knees below his short pants, bare above dark socks.

"I wanted long pants," he said, suddenly sad. "I look goofy."

"I look like a tulip," Jazz told him. She smoothed her best yellow dress. "Maybe a daffodil. A very pretty daffodil."

"Kids! Let's roll out!" Grandpa called from downstairs. He was always ready first.

Rosalind rushed into Koo's room. "I told him I'd check on you two," she said. Rosalind was round and sweet-looking, and the steam from Jazz's and Koo's baths had made her cheeks as red as a scarlet parrot.

"I look goofy," Koo told Rosalind. She straightened his tie with one quick tug. She smoothed his hair flat in two pats. She made a wrinkle in his jacket disappear with three wipes of her damp apron.

"He looks goofy," Jazz agreed. "But *I* look like a tulip."

"You both look late by your grandfather's watch," Rosalind said.

Jazz walked carefully past Rosalind, into the hallway.

"I look nice?" Koo asked himself in the mirror. He polished the toe of one shoe on the sock of his other leg.

"Koo," Jazz whispered from the hallway, "you do look nice. Now come on." He smiled, and they both galloped downstairs and then out the door with Grandpa, where Ben was waiting to drive them all to the restaurant.

Koo recognized the restaurant by the smooth white door between two tall pillars. Above the door was a sign in blue and gold that said THE WATERWORKS. As they went inside, Jazz saw the man who always wore a white suit with gold braid crisscrossing the front. Jazz liked the way he bobbed his head and clicked his heels.

"Mr. Putter—delighted—right this way," the man said, coming up to them. "Young lady—charmed; you, too, young man—sir." Jazz waited for him to click his heels. But this time he just bowed, and she and Koo bowed back.

"Good to see you, Carquois," Grandpa Putter said. He tapped Jazz on the shoulder with his cane and then Koo, directing them to

Dressing Up

follow Carquois. But Jazz and Koo knew that before they got to the table Grandpa would wave at or shake hands with nearly every diner he passed.

"Hello, Putter," said someone at the very first table.

"Blakely! There you are. It's the right night to run into you," Grandpa exclaimed, looking at the man's plate. "How's the special?"

"Perfect," Blakely answered.

Neither Jazz nor Koo ever understood just what Grandpa and his friends talked about. It was like the gibberish they heard on radio commercials—lots of noise and static that never made sense.

"I have to get these children to the table," Grandpa said. "See you Monday morning, right?" Blakely nodded and they moved on.

"Good evening, Senator," Grandpa said, patting another man on the back as he passed.

"They all look alike," Jazz whispered to Koo.

"Maybe they all went to the same tailor," Koo whispered back.

"Or the same barber shop," Jazz added. Then she saw a woman sitting at the head of

Dressing Up

a large table touch Grandpa's arm lightly. She wore a white dress, with feathers on her sleeves.

Of all the people Grandpa had greeted, she was the only one Jazz and Koo had never seen before.

"I like *her*," said Koo.

"She looks like a swan," said Jazz.

"With all the other creatures around her," added Koo.

"And they're all in a little pond," Jazz said in a soft voice.

"Minerva—good to see you," Grandpa said. The children just stared.

"Hello, Eugene," she said. "May we count on you for the toy fund?"

"Count me in!" Grandpa Putter said. "The same as last time," he quickly added.

The woman smiled at Jazz and Koo, then up at Grandpa. "I knew I could depend on you." She looked at her empty plate. "The special is wonderful, as always."

"Thanks for the tip," Grandpa Putter answered. "Come, children. Carquois has our regular spot ready."

They sat down by a window, Grandpa taking

his favorite chair. They could see the entire restaurant and the front door. Koo watched the waiters and waitresses slam in and out of the swinging door of the kitchen, their heavy loads held high overhead or stacked on carts. Jazz faced a huge painting of an old water mill. Deer and rabbits and bears sipped from a bubbling stream. It was a happy picture.

"Would you like to start with—would you like something to drink?" Carquois asked them. "Eh—the usual?" he asked Grandpa.

"Yes, thank you, Carquois," Grandpa Putter told him.

"And perhaps the children would be interested in knowing that we have plenty of fancies on our dessert cart this evening," he said. "Of course, I mustn't rush you. Your drinks?" He looked at Jazz and Koo.

"I want a Roy Rogers," Koo told him.

"And I'll have a Shirley Temple," Jazz said.

"Of course. I'll send your waiter right over with them." Carquois left, and a basket of rolls appeared before them, fragrant and warm beneath a clean white napkin. Pads of butter were arranged on top of crushed ice in a silver bowl. Then the waiter brought their drinks.

Dressing Up

Koo sipped his drink. It was a dark cola with a bright red cherry, but it came in a glass just like the one used for Grandpa's drink—a small bowl on top of a tall stem.

Jazz sipped hers. It was only cherry syrup with fizzy soda in it, but she loved the little umbrella that poked out of the glass.

"Tarnation!" Grandpa Putter said. "Is that your grandmother headed this way?"

He was staring out the window at Granny Hoe, who knocked on the glass from the sidewalk. She waved at them, and Jazz and Koo could see her lips move. Jazz knew from Granny's muddy clothes that she had been gardening after the store closed.

Grandpa Putter looked away from the window with his hand shielding his face. "She's not coming in here dressed like that, is she?" he grumbled.

"I think so," Koo said. He eagerly watched the door.

"I hope so," Jazz said quietly. She sipped her drink and tried not to watch the door like Koo.

Grandpa didn't say anything, but his face turned red as he peeked at the door.

Granny Hoe did not come in.

"I think we've been spared," Grandpa told them at last. He beamed. "Now, let's order." Without moving more than his eyebrow, Grandpa made the waiter come to the table.

"Your favorite game hen, Mr. Putter, is one of our main attractions this evening," the waiter said. "There is also some good quail, and of course the special."

"I think we'll go for three of the evening's special, Carquois," Grandpa said.

"With french fries," Koo said. He was sure that this man was not Carquois, but Grandpa seemed so certain.

"And milk shakes," Jazz added. She wondered if everyone who worked in the restaurant was named Carquois. Grandpa always seemed to think so.

The waiter frowned. "The hoozy for the french fries has gone kerflooey. But the milk shakes are coming right up."

"And some of your red wine with dinner— you know, the smooth stuff," Grandpa added.

The waiter said, "A bottle of . . ." and made a musical noise with his words.

Dressing Up

Grandpa answered, "Sure, sure, that's it."

"But of course." The waiter left them.

"Did he say 'Ta-ti-TON, tan-ton'?" Jazz asked Koo.

"No, he said 'Ta-ti-TONE, toot-toot,' " Koo replied. "That's what he always says, right, Grandpa?"

"Oh, I never bit into that dor-may-voo stuff," Grandpa answered. "But your grandmother— Grandma Putter, that is—she spoke French like a singsong bird."

Koo sat up in his seat. "Granny!" he said, pointing at the kitchen. Both Grandpa and Jazz turned in their chairs in time to see Granny Hoe sail out of the kitchen with her arms full of brown bags.

"Hello, good citizens," she cried. She made her way toward their table. "Hello, children."

Grandpa quickly stood up as she approached, and then just as quickly sat down. Granny pulled the spare chair out from the table and put the brown bags on it. "Ooof. You wouldn't think bread would be so heavy."

"What's the bread for?" Jazz asked.

"Did you buy it?" Koo wanted to know.

"Now, really," Grandpa Putter said, "do you have to spread your bags all over—we're trying to have some peaceful fun."

"It's for the soup kitchen," Granny said. "And no, I didn't have to buy it. Cook Bernie always makes extra for me."

"We're having the special," Koo said.

"But the hoozy for the french fries went kerflooey, so we're only having milk shakes," Jazz told her.

"My good woman," Grandpa said, "the children will be at your house all weekend. Now please let us have our evening to ourselves."

Granny didn't hear him. She looked around the restaurant. "Bah! You wouldn't catch me eating the overpriced canned food here." She brushed some dirt off one of her sleeves. "As much as I like Bernie, there's nothing like good home cooking." She picked up her bags, ready to leave.

The waiter arrived, wheeling a little cart right up to their table. Clash, he put a silver-covered plate down for each of them. Flash, he put the milk shakes in front of Jazz and Koo. Splash, he poured wine into Grandpa Putter's glass.

Dressing Up

Crash, he whisked off the lids and left them staring at . . .

"Raw meat!" Granny said. "Don't eat it unless you have to. Good night, children." Jazz and Koo looked at their own plates. Then they looked at each other's plates. Then they looked at each other. Granny was already out the door.

Koo puckered his mouth up near his nose. "Red," he said.

"And bloody," Jazz added.

"Delightful ground steak," Grandpa said. "Can't remember the official name of this dish, but I assure you, it is delicious." He placed a spoonful of raw beef on a triangle of toast, added chopped onion and a dose of parsley, and popped it in his mouth. He closed his eyes. "Mmmmm." Then he opened his eyes and drank some wine.

When he looked at Jazz and Koo, he saw that they were not eating. They were staring at him.

"May we order dessert?" Koo asked. Jazz nodded.

"Carquois!" Grandpa bellowed. Dash, the real Carquois was by their table.

"Yes—Mr. Putter—what can I do for you—it would be my privilege—is there a problem?"

"Pop these two patties on your grill and bring 'em back as hamburgers," he said.

Koo grinned. Jazz did not.

"With cheese for Jazz," Grandpa added hastily. "And I don't care if the hoozy is ker-whatever—bring these children some oiled potatoes and call them french fries."

This time, Jazz and Koo both smiled. "And don't forget the ketchup, please," Koo said.

"Peach pie, lemon cake, chocolate truffle, candied cupcakes," Jazz said to Rosalind. They both tugged at Jazz's pajamas, trying to get them on over her head.

"Apple brown Betty, mocha tarts, pumpkin fudge, teensy-weensy mints, caramel pears, and *cheese*!" Koo announced. He entered Jazz's room in his pajamas and robe. "Cheese for *dessert*!" he repeated, laughing.

"And we had a taste of most of them," Jazz continued.

"Of all of them," Koo put in.

"Of *most* of them," Jazz repeated.

"Of a couple of them," Koo said.

Dressing Up

"Well, we each chose one," Jazz said.

"But we shared them," Koo told Rosalind.

"My oh my," Rosalind said. "You'll have sweet dreams then." She helped Jazz up to her bed, then took Koo into the next room and tucked him in. They both heard her shuffle down the hall. Her door closed, and the house was silent.

"Jazz?" Koo called from the next room. Jazz could barely hear his voice.

"What?" Jazz asked in a loud whisper.

"Are you sleepy?"

"No, are you?"

"No," Koo answered. "Are you hungry?"

"Yes," Jazz replied. "Are you?"

"Yes," he said.

"What do you want to do?" she asked.

"You want to go downstairs?"

"Yes," she said. She climbed out of bed and put on her bathrobe and slippers. They tiptoed quietly down the stairs. There was no sound from Grandpa's room, at one end of the hall. There was no sound from Rosalind's, at the other.

A light glowed beneath the den door. "Grandpa's in there," Koo said. They knew he often read the newspaper late at night, after everyone else was in bed.

Jazz said, "I have a hot-dog smell in my nose."

Koo put his finger to his lips. "Me too," he said. He pointed toward the kitchen. They tried to be quiet as they moved down the hall. The hot-dog smell was getting stronger.

The kitchen was empty, except for a plastic wrapper from a package of hot-dog buns on the counter.

Jazz could see the flames of a fire just outside the kitchen window.

"The house is on fire," Koo said.

Jazz shook her head.

"What is it?" he whispered.

"Someone must be out there," Jazz said.

"We should get Grandpa," Koo suggested.

"No, we'll have to go ourselves," Jazz said. She tried to remind herself that she was brave. "We're not supposed to be up."

They went out the kitchen door, into the garage. Their hearts were racing faster than Granny Hoe's sewing machine.

The back door of the garage had a window.

Dressing Up

They could see someone wrapped in a blanket, leaning over the fire. It was darker than Granny Hoe's root cellar, and they could just make out the circle of rocks around the fire in a bed of garden dirt.

"That's Grandmother Putter's quilt, with the squares and circles," Jazz whispered.

"From the couch in the den," Koo reminded her.

Jazz was pretty sure she knew who was outside.

So did Koo.

She opened the door.

He cried, "Who's there?"

Grandpa answered, "It's only me. Why are you two still up?" He was sitting on a patio chair he had pulled up to the fire. A hot dog on a stick was sizzling over the flames.

Koo stepped forward. "We're hungry."

Grandpa laughed. "I know," he said. "Me too." He waved a stick at them.

Jazz shivered in the cool spring air and moved closer to the fire.

Grandpa balanced the stick over the flame and held open the blanket. Jazz went under his right arm. Koo went under his left arm. The three of them huddled by the fire while the hot dog finished cooking.

"Why didn't you just fix a sandwich?" Koo asked.

"Well, when my—your grandmother—was alive, we used to go camping," Grandpa said. "I miss it—the cooking, the outdoors. And her, too."

"Tonight?" Jazz asked. "Why?"

"Something your Granny Hoe said," Grandpa told her. "She was right—there's nothing like home-cooked food."

"Is this home-cooked food?" Jazz asked.

"Tarnation!" Grandpa said. "We're home. I'm cooking. What else could it be!"

Jazz giggled. Koo yawned.

"One hot dog each," Grandpa Putter said, putting two more hot dogs on his stick. "And then all good campers need shut-eye."

Buying Trees

Granny Hoe's truck bangeddy-banged over the potholes in front of Grandpa Putter's house. She didn't turn into the driveway but stopped the truck in the street with the motor running. Jazz and Koo ran across the lawn.

"I can only go forward today—the truck won't back up!" she yelled over the noisy engine.

"Where are we going?" Koo asked, sitting next to the window.

"Out to the nursery by the river," Granny Hoe answered. "I want to buy new fruit trees for my garden. Do you have your swimsuits like I told you?"

Koo nodded.

Jazz patted her shirt. "Under our clothes," she said.

"Good," said Granny. "Buying saplings is hot work, even this late in the afternoon. We'll want to cool off. The store was too warm all day, and it's barely June." They put-putted down the road, until Grandpa's house was out of sight.

Just then, a huge white car roared by them, sending up dust that went into the truck's open windows and settled on their clothes. "That was your Grandpa Putter," Granny said, "with Ben at the wheel. Bah! You wouldn't catch me letting someone else drive me around."

Jazz and Koo were silent. "Ben and Grandpa were in a war together," Jazz finally said.

"Across the ocean," Koo said. He thought about his parents. But they weren't in a war.

"We missed the turn!" Granny exclaimed.

"You have to back up," Koo said.

"I can't, remember?" Granny answered. "We'll have to go around the block."

At last they were headed down the brown dirt road that took them to the nursery and the river.

Buying Trees

The nursery was a small red house with white trim and rows of small potted trees out front. A greenhouse was attached to one side.

While Granny Hoe chose her trees, Jazz and Koo circled around some evergreens that looked like a real forest, and then went behind the red house to the river.

"Don't go *in* the river," Granny Hoe called to them. "You can dangle your feet while you wait for me."

The water looked cool. A small rowboat was moored on the other side. "It's Grandpa's boat," Jazz cried.

"Halloooo," Koo called.

"Grandpa, it's us!" Jazz yelled. But Grandpa was too far away to hear them. Jazz and Koo sat by the river and splashed their legs.

"I can swim," Koo said, paddling his hands through the air.

"You can wade," Jazz said. "I can swim."

"We can all swim," Granny said, coming up behind them with beach towels. She had put the new trees in her truck. The sun was sinking lower in the sky.

Jazz and Koo spread out the towels. Granny held first Jazz, and then Koo, around the waist while they practiced swim strokes in the shallow water.

"Is that your Grandpa Putter out there?" she asked.

"Yes," Jazz said, "but he can't hear us."

"Bah! Nothing'll bite in *these* waters," Granny said. "He should leave the little fish alone."

They finished swimming and folded up their towels and left. But while Granny was driving down the brown dirt road, the truck groaned to a stop and then was silent.

"Bah!" Granny Hoe said again. She got out of the truck. She opened the hood. She bent over the engine. She slammed the hood shut.

"What's wrong, Granny?" Koo asked. He slid behind the wheel and honked the horn.

"It's simple," Granny told him, leaning through the window. "First the truck didn't go backward. Now it doesn't go forward."

Jazz got out of the truck and made shade for the saplings by hooking up her beach towel like an awning. The leaves had curled earlier, in the heat of the day. Even though the sun would be going down soon, the air still felt hot.

She knew they were stuck.

Koo honked the horn again.

A long white car pulled up next to them.

"Need some help?" Ben asked.

"Climb in!" Grandpa Putter yelled. "Lucky we came along."

Granny Hoe harrumphed. "I can fix my truck—eventually. But I've got hot children and wilted saplings to worry about."

"Ben will drive all of you home," Grandpa Putter told them.

"I've done my own driving for plenty of years," Granny muttered. "Koo, get out of that truck. Children, you go along. Mr. Putter, would you kindly call a mechanic for me?"

Jazz tugged Granny Hoe's hand.

Koo said, "Please come—it's going to get dark."

Granny grumbled, but she got in the car.

"I hate being a passenger," she said.

The car went a few yards, then sputtered to a stop.

"Tarnation!" Grandpa yelled. "Ben, can you fix it?"

Ben got out and banged the door shut. But

he returned after only a quick look under the hood of the car, which he left up.

"I don't know what's wrong," Ben said through the open window. "I can walk into town."

Granny Hoe peered over the back seat. "If I fix this chariot, can I drive us home?"

"Sure," Grandpa Putter said, winking at Jazz and Koo.

"I'll have to get my tools out of the truck," Granny said. She left the car and Ben got back in.

Granny was gone a long time. When she returned, darkness had settled over them. Ben called, "Do you need help?" but Granny didn't answer. They could not see what she was doing.

"No, thank you," she answered at last. She tinkered around at the side, slammed the hood, and waited while Ben climbed out of the driver's seat and into the back with Jazz and Koo. Granny Hoe slid behind the wheel.

The car started right up.

"Hurray!" said Jazz and Koo.

"How did you do that?" asked Grandpa Putter.

"It's no secret," Granny Hoe answered. "My truck isn't fancy, but when *I'm* driving, I always try to have a full tank of gas."

On the way home, Granny was glad to be driving but wished that she were in her truck.

Grandpa wished that Ben were driving.

Ben wished there were more room in the back seat for his long legs.

And Jazz and Koo wished that the ride home were longer, because, for once, they were all in one car.

Do-gooding

Jazz and Koo sat in their pajamas on the floor next to Koo's bed. "Grandpa Putter is late to read to us tonight," he said, running his hand like a car along the carpet trim.

"Koo," Jazz said, throwing her storybook on the bed, "what should we do about Binney?"

"Who is Binney?" he asked.

"That ragtag woman—you *know*!" she said.

Koo thought. Then he remembered. Yesterday they had gone grocery shopping with Granny Hoe. Outside the store, Granny Hoe had talked to an old woman. Granny called her Binney. Koo had liked her red sneakers. He had red sneakers, too. But Binney's were dirty and twisted. Her frizzy blue hair stuck out from her torn knit bonnet, and she had hugged a frayed sweater around her chest. Behind her was a red metal wagon that she was pulling with a rope.

Granny had taken all the cheese from her shopping bag and handed it to Binney. Then she pulled out a bag of apples and gave that to her as well. Jazz and Koo had watched the old woman shuffle down the street, her wagon rattling behind her.

"These days I see Binney at the City Shelter," Granny had told them. "She takes some meals at the soup kitchen there. But her family was well known in this town when I was young."

"I asked Grandpa and he told me to ask you," Koo had interrupted. "How much do you get paid for working there?"

"I don't," Granny had said.

"Why not?" Jazz had asked.

"Because there are too many people like Binney," Granny had said. It hadn't been a very satisfying answer.

Now Koo answered, moving his car-hand

around a curve on the carpet. "I don't know what we should do," he said. "What do you mean?" He liked Binney's name. The same name was on the bottom of his lunch box. In tiny print.

"Granny said she's really poor and hungry," Jazz said.

"But Granny gave her our cheese," Koo said. "We had to eat bologna sandwiches."

"Koo," Jazz said, "just apples and cheese— that's all she had to eat."

"Granny said that it would be a feast for Binney," Koo protested. "Wait! I know—we should have a real feast for her. A picnic; and we'll invite her, and Granny and Grandpa and Ben and Rosalind—"

"You're right," Jazz said. "A picnic would be good. But it should be a secret picnic."

Koo sat up. "No one would know?" he asked. "Why?"

"I just don't think we should tell," Jazz answered. "Maybe it's a stupid plan."

"It's not," Koo told her. "We'll get Ben to help."

Jazz leaned against the bed. "Tomorrow after

school. We'll wait until Rosalind is out of the kitchen."

"A big picnic," Koo added. "Just for Binney."

"A huge and delicious picnic," Jazz replied.

"Aha!" Grandpa Putter said, coming into Koo's room. "A huge and delicious what?"

Had he heard them?

"Nothing, Grandpa," Jazz said. Grandpa lifted her off the floor.

"Really, Grandpa," Koo said, climbing into bed. "We were just talking about a huge and delicious bedtime story." Koo leaned over and switched on his clown night-light. "You promised."

"What do *you* want to make?" Koo asked Jazz in the kitchen the next day.

"I don't know, what do *you* want to make?" Jazz asked him in return.

"Well, when I'm extra hungry, I like chocolate," Koo told her.

"No. Chocolate gets sickening," Jazz said. "I mean, if you have too much. Granny Hoe said so."

Do-gooding

"Okay, what do you like when you're just plain hungry?" Koo asked her.

"Plain hungry? A mountain of mashed potatoes, roast goose, gravy, cranberry sauce, pumpkin pie," Jazz replied.

"We can't make all that!" Koo protested.

"I know," Jazz told him. "But you asked me what I like when I'm plain hungry."

Koo sat down on the floor. "Jazz! Come on! We have to think of something."

"We can make chocolate milk," Jazz said, sitting down next to him, "and put it in a thermos. That's not sickening."

"Okay," Koo said. "But that's not something you eat."

"Ham and Swiss-cheese sandwiches," Jazz added. She stood up, pulled open the refrigerator door, and peeked inside. "Plenty here."

"Is peanut butter and jelly too easy?" Koo asked her, looking over her shoulder.

"Baby stuff! Tuna fish, ham salad," Jazz said. "Lots of that." Even though Grandpa ate out a lot, he insisted that Rosalind keep the refrigerator full for lunches, snacks, and picnics.

"Cold chicken, roast beef," Koo chanted. He

pulled a shopping bag out of a cupboard and wrapped up a whole platter of cold chicken. "Enough for two picnics!" he said, putting it in the bag.

Jazz packed the roast beef into a piece of foil and slipped that in the bag, too. "Potato chips, celery sticks, sliced carrots, pickles," she sang. "Next?" She kept putting food in the middle of the floor.

"Cupcakes, bananas, fruit salad," Koo said.

"Tiny fish eggs—yuck! Salmon—maybe! Cookies, cake, and ice cream—yes, yes, yes," Jazz added.

"STOP!" Koo cried. "Not ice cream. It would melt."

Jazz nodded and pushed the ice cream back into the freezer. Then she pulled out another shopping bag, because the first one was full. When everything was packed, they sat back and looked at their work.

"That's it," said Jazz.

"Yup. Perfect," Koo agreed.

"But there is just one problem," Jazz said.

"We didn't ask Ben to drive us to Binney," Koo said.

Do-gooding

"Did I hear my name?" Ben said, stepping into the kitchen.

"Ben!" Koo said. "Can you take us on an errand?"

"And don't ask any questions!" Jazz warned him.

"I'll take you on your errand," Ben told Koo. He turned to Jazz. "And my lips are sealed."

"Okay?" Koo asked Jazz.

"Okay," she replied. "Time to go?"

"Ready—" Koo said, "or not!"

Jazz and Koo sat in the front seat. They took turns checking on the shopping bags in the back seat.

They were in the car for a long time, making Ben drive down every street in town. But they didn't see Binney.

"Listen, youngsters," Ben finally said. "Where are you taking me? We've been driving around in circles. We passed by the toy store three times and you didn't ask to go in once. And the old man is going to worry if we aren't home when he arrives."

"We don't want toys, silly Ben," Jazz said.

Then she shrieked. "Stop! Stop! Slow the car down!"

"Wait a minute," Koo said. "Stop, Ben! Please! Jazz is right! Over there, by the old bridge!"

"I really think this has gone far enough," Ben said, slowing the car down slightly. "I helped you load up the car, without your grandpa's permission. Now what?" He pulled the car over to the curb and turned it off.

Jazz and Koo scrambled out of the car. They walked hand in hand. They slowed down as they approached the old woman. Jazz spoke first.

"I'm Jazz," she said. "This is my brother, Koo." Koo pulled on Jazz's hand, ready to leap back to the car at any moment. Ben watched from the rearview mirror.

"Jazz and Koo," Binney mumbled. They saw the smudgy dirt on her face and hands. "Well well, then," she said to them. "Well, hello, Jazz and Koo."

"Why are you wearing a sweater?" Jazz asked. "It's hot out."

"Oh yes, dear me, so I am, so it is. Old bones like mine are never warm," Binney said.

Do-gooding

"What are you young mites up to on this fine day?"

"We brought you stuff," Jazz said. "I'll go help Ben." She ran to the car.

Koo felt shy. "We have the same shoes," he said. He walked two steps backward. He pointed to his feet.

"I see that. Only I bet yours run faster than mine do," Binney said. "Say, I saw you yesterday, didn't I?"

"With our granny," Koo said, nodding.

"Little Jeannie Hoe—this is her doing. Sending her young ones on the rounds. She's a fine woman. Always has been," Binney said.

"You should tell our Grandpa Putter that," Koo told her. "He and Granny fight all the time."

"You say Putter is your grandpa?" Binney asked.

"Yes," Jazz said, dragging one of the shopping bags with her. "Grandpa Putter—do you know him?"

"A long long time ago, *I'd* say that was," Binney said. "A hundred years ago."

Koo giggled. "He was a *baby* a hundred years ago," he said.

"That's when I knew him all right," Binney said, scratching her ear. "Too bad he didn't stay a baby."

Jazz took Koo's hand. "This is for you," she said, handing Binney the shopping bag.

"You know I wouldn't take charity from your grandpa," Binney said. "And he knows it, too."

"No, no," Koo said.

"*This* picnic is one of *our* picnics," Jazz said. "But you're having it instead. Koo, get the other bag." Koo scampered over to Ben. He had gotten out of the car and had the other shopping bag with him.

"I really should say I can't take this," Binney said, waving at the bags. "Taking from kids, you know. My." Jazz quit smiling.

"Hello, Binney," Ben said. He put the heavy bag on the ground next to Koo and returned to the car.

"You *have* to take it. It's a picnic," Jazz said. "We packed it up and everything. And we have a thermos of chocolate milk for you."

"We may get in trouble for this," Koo said, looking at Jazz bashfully. He stuttered once,

then started again. "If we go back with this stuff and—"

"Everyone likes picnics, don't they?" Jazz added. "We have them all the time."

"I wouldn't want you to be in trouble on *my* account," Binney said. She put the bags into her red wagon and then stared, first at her own sneakers and then at Koo's. She smiled at Jazz. "And I thank you," she said.

In the car Jazz looked at Ben. He hadn't spoken to them yet and they were almost home.

"Rosalind *always* lets us take picnics from the refrigerator," she reminded him.

"That's true," Ben said. "But don't you think this was at least a couple of picnics?"

"Sure," Koo answered.

"We'll just skip two picnics," Jazz said.

"You will?" Ben said.

Koo nudged Jazz. She nodded.

"Looks like there won't be any picnics for a long while," Ben told them, driving slowly into the garage.

"Nope," Jazz said. She took Koo's arm. "No more picnics—until the Fourth of July, that is."

"Not until the Fourth of July," Koo echoed.

Do-gooding

The three of them walked into Grandpa Putter's house. And then stopped.

Rosalind was wailing. "The refrigerator is practically empty!" she said.

"Calm down," Grandpa Putter told her.

"Carting away that much stuff . . ."

"Jazz and Koo move in mysterious ways," Grandpa Putter replied. "Just phone the grocery store and tell Sam to deliver whatever you need." He turned and saw Jazz and Koo with Ben. "Where have *you* been?" he asked.

"With Ben," Koo said, looking at Jazz.

"And where have *you* been?" Grandpa asked Ben.

"With the children," Ben replied, standing alongside Koo and holding Jazz's hand.

"And where were all of you?" Grandpa asked again.

Jazz spoke up. "We were near the toy store," she said. "But we couldn't afford anything."

"That's right—we couldn't afford anything so we decided to come to you for help," said Ben seriously. "But I'll take them back tomorrow—if they have some spending money."

"I guess I know a conspiracy when I see

one," Grandpa said, rubbing his duck-head cane. "Well, Ben, don't you owe me money from our cream-puff tennis match last week?"

Ben nodded.

"You can use that," Grandpa Putter said, grinning.

Ben hesitated for a moment, then said, "Double or nothing! We'll play a new game tomorrow morning."

"Agreed," Grandpa said, laughing.

"Money for Binney, *and* money for toys," Koo whispered to Jazz.

"Agreed," said Jazz.

Getting Sick

A few days before school was out for the summer, Jazz put her head down on her desk during class.

Her eyes watered and her forehead ached. Luckily, her teacher noticed and sent her to the nurse. Koo watched her leave the classroom. He didn't feel very well, either. Maybe.

"I have to send you home," the nurse said to Jazz. "I'll call your parents to come get you."

Jazz wanted to cry. "My parents aren't home," she said. "They're on a trip."

"Who *can* take you home?" the nurse asked.

Jazz said, "Grandpa Putter," and told her the phone number. But no one was at Grandpa's house, not even Rosalind or Ben. Jazz felt terrible.

"Who else can we call?" the nurse asked.

"Granny Hoe," Jazz replied. She curled up in a ball on the cot and held on to a pillow. That helped. "At the hardware store."

Not too many minutes later, Granny Hoe sailed into the nurse's office. Jazz cried a little. Just a little. "There there, now, you'll be all right." Granny wrapped a shawl around Jazz. "I'll take good care of you."

"Someone should tell Koo," Jazz said. Granny Hoe looked at the nurse. The nurse looked at Jazz. Jazz knew she would feel awful if no one told her where Koo had gone.

"I'll tell your teacher," the nurse said. "She'll tell Koo."

"And Koo will tell Ben when he picks him up after school," Granny Hoe added.

Soon they were in the front seat of the truck, bumping toward Granny Hoe's house. Jazz felt worse because she was sick, but better because she was with her granny.

"What about the store?" Jazz asked suddenly.

"I closed it up," Granny told her.

Getting Sick

"What about the customers?" Jazz asked.

"I, too, make signs," Granny Hoe answered. "This one says JAZZ IS SICK. My good customers will understand. My bad customers—bah!"

At her house, Granny threw a bright patchwork quilt on the couch. She stuffed clean pillows into the corners, and when Jazz lay down, the cloth felt cool against her skin. Granny pulled another quilt up to Jazz's chin. She brought her a mug of hot lemonade with a cinnamon stick and an old box of paper dolls. Then Granny Hoe sat down at the piano by the wall and played songs. When she hit the high notes with a squeak, Jazz giggled.

At 4:00 they heard the doorbell. Granny Hoe opened the door and Koo was standing there. Grandpa Putter was right behind him. "Are you all right?" Koo asked as they came into Granny's house.

Jazz was sniffly, but she smiled. "I'm fine."

"I was worried when you left, you know. Sort of. They told me you'd gone home," Koo said.

"I didn't know you were sick, Jazz. I'm sorry," Grandpa Putter said. He sat down on the couch next to her, even though there was not much room for him. "I was helping raise money for the Toy and Doll Museum I told you about."

He touched her warm head.

"She should stay here," he said to Granny. "I can send Rosalind over to help you."

"I don't need any help," Granny answered.

"But what about your store?" Grandpa Putter asked.

"Bah!" said Granny Hoe. She took Jazz's empty mug to the kitchen.

"What about *me*?" Koo asked, looking at Jazz. They had never been separated for the night. Maybe it would be different without Jazz down the hall from his room. "You don't have your night-light," he added.

"Now now," Grandpa said, putting his arm around Koo's shoulder. "We'll go home and keep *you* well there. And Jazz will feel better in no time." Koo shrugged. He wasn't so sure.

That night, Jazz couldn't sleep. "Granny!" she called into the darkness surrounding her bed.

"I'm here," Granny said, coming into Jazz's room. The hall light blazed around her head. "What's wrong?" she asked.

"I don't know," Jazz replied, sniffling. "I just can't sleep."

Granny went over to the wall that faced Jazz's bed. Suddenly the room was lighted by a rosy glow. Jazz looked at the wall. A clown night-light smiled at her. She smiled back.

"I always keep an extra night-light around here," Granny told her. "Sometimes *I* can't sleep."

That night, Koo couldn't sleep, either. "Grandpa!" he called. Grandpa came into the room, his bathrobe trailing behind him and his sleeves flapping like wings.

"Yes, Koo?" he asked. "Shall we read a story together?"

"I don't think so," Koo said. He pointed to the clown night-light by his bed. "It's keeping me awake."

Grandpa snapped it off, and the room dimmed. Then he kissed Koo's forehead and left.

Koo snuggled into the sheets. He slept.

In four days, Jazz was well. And Granny Hoe was ready to open her store again. She and Jazz went early to get ready for Saturday's customers. But the store was already open!

Getting Sick

Ben was dusting the shelves, Koo was at the cash register, and Grandpa Putter was sweeping.

Koo rushed up to Jazz. "I missed you—I mean, everyone at school missed you," he told her.

"And I missed everybody," Jazz said. "The last week of school is always the best."

"Look at Grandpa's red face," Koo said. "He must be really mad."

Together they watched Grandpa Putter while Granny Hoe stared at him. Something was different. Grandpa didn't seem mad—he seemed uncomfortable.

"Koo showed me where you keep your extra key," Grandpa said hurriedly. "And we showed the customers your sign." He pointed, and Jazz saw the sign that said JAZZ IS SICK.

"Evvvveryone's been helping this week," he stuttered. "Aaaand it's all in order."

Granny Hoe still hadn't spoken. Jazz thought she was angry.

Grandpa Putter seemed to think so, too. "And tonight I'll take us all to dinner," he said in a rush.

"No," Granny Hoe answered. Koo and Jazz

still didn't know what to think. Was it going to be another fight?

"Tonight," Granny Hoe told them, "I'll cook dinner for Jazz and Koo—and you."

"A home-cooked meal," Grandpa Putter said, smiling. His face wasn't red anymore—it was pink. "After a good day's work, that would be just the thing."

Quarreling

Granny's tomato seeds had washed away in a rainstorm. But she would need tomatoes in the fall. So on Sunday morning, Jazz and Koo helped her place small green plants where the seeds used to be.

Jazz dug a hole. Koo put a tomato plant into the hole. Jazz smoothed the dirt around the plant, press, press, press. And Koo made the next hole, dig, dig, dig. Back and forth, taking turns, they had almost finished one row.

"I want to plant flowers," Koo said.

"It's a small garden," Jazz told him. "Granny says there's only room for food plants. And we still have to plant the sweet potatoes."

"Yoo-hoo!" Granny Hoe called from her small grove of new fruit trees. She was putting stakes next to each one, so they would grow as straight and tall as the other trees.

"We'll stop in a while," she said. She watered the ground around the roots of the saplings. Granny knew the trees needed both sun and water, never too much of either.

When the sun was too high in the sky for work, Granny brought them cold cranberry juice and lemonade to sip in the shade.

"How much more do we have to do?" Granny asked them. "Are you tired yet?"

Jazz shook her head no.

Koo nodded yes.

Just then they heard the neep-neep of Grandpa Putter's horn. He was supposed to drive Jazz and Koo back to his house, but not until later in the day.

Soon he and Ben were also sitting in the shade, with cold juice to drink.

"What brings you here so early, Mr. Putter?" Granny Hoe asked.

"I've been thinking about the trees you bought," Grandpa answered.

Quarreling

Koo tugged on Grandpa's sleeve. "They're over there," he told him, pointing.

"I decided you needed some flowers, too," Grandpa Putter announced. "Ben, get them out of the car."

"Hurray!" Koo cried. "Flowers smell nice."

"No," Jazz said. "Granny says there's no room."

"Thank you, but I don't have very much land," Granny told him. "I grow vegetables for canning and fruit for jam. I sell them in the store."

"I won't take no for an answer," Grandpa told her. "I bought these flowers just for you."

"I don't care. I don't like being told how to garden," Granny answered.

"I like flowers," Koo said, taking Grandpa's hand.

"I want fruit jam," Jazz told him, crossing her arms and moving closer to Granny Hoe.

"There's a strip of dirt running along the fence," Ben pointed out. "Flowers wouldn't take away from the vegetables."

Jazz and Koo ran over to the fence. Granny came over next to consider it. Then Grandpa.

Ben went to the car and returned with several blossoming plants.

"You need more room for all the flowers I brought," Grandpa Putter said. "That little strip is too small."

"Stop your interfering," Granny Hoe said. "Why don't you just sit down in the shade and have another cool drink." She led him back over to the chairs.

"My sweet potatoes were supposed to go here!" Jazz said to Koo.

"We have flowers!" Koo answered. "And I don't *like* sweet potatoes!"

"Bah! It's not your garden!" Jazz yelled.

"Tarnation! It's not yours, either," Koo yelled back.

He picked up the watering can and dumped water on Jazz.

She grabbed the sprinkler and aimed it at him. They were both drenched and muddy.

Jazz hit Koo.

Koo hit back.

Grandpa Putter grabbed Jazz just as she kicked Koo.

Koo started to bite her, but Granny Hoe pulled him out of the way first.

Jazz and Koo stopped fighting when they saw that both Granny and Grandpa were laughing at them.

"We have to get back to work on the tomato plants," Granny said, wiping her eyes. "I suppose a few flowers along the fence would be fine."

"Ben," Grandpa said, shaking his head, "plant the flowers here. Then it's time to get Jazz and Koo to Rosalind for an early supper."

"Sorry, I'm off duty," Ben replied. "But I'll drive the children home and come back for you later."

Muddy and mad at each other, Jazz and Koo climbed into Grandpa Putter's clean white car. Suddenly the seats were not white anymore.

Grandpa was staring at Ben. "The flowers will wilt unless someone plants them," he sputtered.

"I have an extra pair of overalls," Granny said, looking at Grandpa Putter's white suit.

"But I have to get to my club for dinner!" Grandpa declared.

"First you plant," Granny told him. "You brought me flowers, which I accept. But I didn't agree to plant them."

Quarreling

Grandpa shook his head one more time, but he hurried into Granny Hoe's house and changed into the overalls. Soon he was back in the yard.

"See you in a little while," Grandpa called to Ben, who was sitting in the driver's seat. "Otherwise I'll have to ride home in that rattletrap truck." He went over to the fence and picked up the shovel.

"You should be so lucky," Granny Hoe grumbled.

"Why do they have to fight all the time?" Koo asked Ben from the back seat.

"Look who's talking," Jazz said.

"Because, unlike you two, they don't know how to talk to each other any other way," Ben replied, starting the car. "It's like a bad habit."

"Like sucking your thumb when you're a baby?" Koo asked.

"Something like that," Ben said. "Their differences go way back, that's for sure. I don't remember what started them off. I bet *they* don't remember, either."

"But does that mean they're going to get a divorce?" Jazz asked.

"Nah, people who have never been married

can't get a divorce," Ben told her. He let the engine warm up.

"Mom and Dad are married. Are they getting a divorce on their trip?" asked Koo.

Ben turned around. "Where'd you get *that* idea from?" he asked them.

"From me," said Jazz. "I told him."

"Why?" Ben asked. "Do your parents fight?"

"No," Koo replied.

"At school I heard that parents go away when they get a divorce," Jazz told Ben. "Our parents went away."

"Well, what I say is that people don't go away together to get a divorce, although they might go away to prevent one," Ben replied. The car started to move. "Your parents are traveling on business. And that's all."

"What are you babbling about over there?" they heard Granny Hoe say to Grandpa Putter. Ben made the car go faster. Jazz and Koo peered out the rear window, watching Granny Hoe's house grow smaller. Two tiny figures were bending over the little patch of land by the fence, arguing.

Marching
and Dancing

"Veet-dee-dee-dee-dee *dum*! Veet dee-dee-dee-dee *dum*!" Jazz sang. She was trying to sound like a trumpet. She still hadn't decided whether to twirl a baton or ride her bike in the Founders' Day parade.

"One-two-three, bend knees," Koo muttered to himself. He was trying to remember something. "One-two-three, bow." He tied paper streamers to the handlebars of his bike. Just like Jazz.

Granny Hoe had finally taken off the training wheels for Koo just a few days ago. He still wasn't sure he could stay balanced. "One-two-three, change partners, swing around," he added.

"What did you say?" Jazz asked.

"I said—oh, I lost count!" he replied. "I was hoping to remember the steps."

"For the dance later?" Jazz asked him. "Baby stuff. You'll remember." She plucked the paper ribbon from the ground and then wound it around her handlebars. Maybe she would ride her bike *and* twirl her baton—at the same time.

Koo was finished. The wheels of his bike looked like twin lollipops. Streamers wove through the spokes. When the bike rolled forward, dizzy pinwheels spun around.

Jazz taped the last ribbon into place. Red pompons also decorated the back of her bike seat, each handlebar, and both ends of her baton.

"You sure'll make a splash with those bikes!" Granny Hoe said, stepping over the low garden fence. "I'll wash my hands and then we'll head out."

"Ready or not!" Koo yelled, climbing on his bike.

"Time to go!" Jazz cried, twirling her baton.

Marching and Dancing

• • •

At the parade Jazz tried hard to twirl her baton and ride her bike at the same time. But she needed one hand for the baton and two hands to steer the bike. She didn't want to crash into the other bikes in the parade.

"I'll take the baton for you," Granny yelled from the sidewalk. "Just until you need it."

"Okay," Jazz said sadly. She handed Granny Hoe the baton. Granny stepped back on the curb and waved her white calico bonnet at them. She wore a fringed skirt and a gingham blouse. The adults were dressed up in what Granny called pioneer clothes.

"I don't see Grandpa," Koo said, wobbling on his bike.

"He's marching with his buddies, in uniform," Jazz said. Koo bent low over his handlebars and pedaled faster. It was easier to balance the bike at that speed, as long as he didn't hit the other children.

"Wait!" Granny Hoe called, running alongside them and pointing with the baton. "Where are you going?"

"To find Grandpa!" Jazz said, following Koo.

They left the other children on bikes behind and pedaled through the marchers.

Jazz rode right up to the drummer in the band. Koo stayed next to the tuba player.

"I see him," Koo cried. "He looks pretty!"

"It's a good thing we helped him sew on his buttons," Jazz declared.

Grandpa Putter had his orange uniform on. It looked pressed and crisp and straight as a brand-new crayon. But the buttons were as crooked as dot-to-dot pictures. Other men marched by his side. They were dressed just like him.

"They're not soldiers," said Koo.

"They're not airplane pilots," said Jazz.

"They're not firemen or doormen or policemen," said Koo.

"Granny says they're Scouts who get to keep the money from the cookies they sell," said Jazz.

"That's not true!" Koo interrupted. "Grandpa says it's his Valentine's Day suit."

"You're wrong!" Jazz protested. "He *says* he wore it at his wedding."

"I want to march," Koo said. "Let's give our bikes to Granny."

Marching and Dancing

"Not yet," Jazz replied. "Granny, I want the baton now!" she called. "I'll hold it the way Grandpa holds his riding crop under his arm," she told Koo.

Granny stood at the curb and tossed the baton high in the air. Up it climbed, down it dropped.

At home, standing still, Jazz could catch the baton every time. But she was on her bike. Her fingers slipped. The baton landed smack in front of the tuba player.

The tuba player skidded on it and tumbled into the drummer.

The drummer tripped over him and knocked Koo off his bike.

The other marchers toppled over next. Jazz rode out of the way.

"Stampede!" the tuba player yelled.

"Stampede!" Koo shrieked.

Granny tried to clear a path. She picked up the baton and poked people with it.

A whistle skewered the air. Jazz clapped her hands over her ears.

"Halt!" Grandpa Putter shouted. "Everyone, calm down! Order, please." Most people stopped. Granny didn't.

"Old bossy," Granny muttered. She shoved through the crowd and found Koo first.

"Tarnation!" Grandpa yelled at her. "Can't you be left with these children for a minute?"

"You old peacock!" Granny Hoe cried. "Preening in your fine feathers." She helped Koo climb over his bike. The front wheel was bent.

"I distinctly was *not* preening!" Grandpa Putter shouted, reaching for Koo at the same time.

"Bunch of old fools," Granny said to herself. "Are you all right?" she said to Koo.

"I'm not hurt," he said. "Maybe I was scared, that's all."

"Crowds can be scary," she admitted. Grandpa dusted off Koo's trousers. Granny waved him away. "Go back to your gosling formation, before they declare you missing in action." But Grandpa stayed by Koo.

Granny brushed Koo's back off and straightened his hair.

"What's gosling tarnation, Granny?" asked Koo.

"Why, gosling *formation* is just walking and quacking, you could say, walkin' 'n' quackin'!"

Granny flapped her arms like a bird. She made Koo laugh.

The fire truck pulled through the middle of the parade. "Everything okay here?" a huge man asked. He had on a black rubber coat. One broad yellow stripe crossed his chest. Two more yellow stripes decorated his big black boots.

"Everything's just fine," answered Grandpa Putter. He patted Jazz on the head. She held her baton. It was bent like Koo's front wheel.

"I'll ride my bike with one hand before the next parade," Jazz said. But she was worried that she was going to need a new baton.

"I'll be able to ride my bike with *no* hands long before that," said Koo. But he was glad that he wouldn't have to ride his bike at all, for now. The wheel was too bent.

"Why don't you load up those bikes on the fire truck," a woman said. She was dressed just like the tall firefighter. "Then follow us to the square. They already have picnic tables set up on the playground." She smiled at Jazz and Koo.

"March?" Koo asked.

Marching and Dancing

Jazz nodded.

Granny nodded.

Grandpa nodded.

"Time to go!" Jazz yelled, taking Granny's hand.

"Ready or not!" Koo cried, marching next to Grandpa.

"Swing your partner left, then right!" called a woman standing on a bale of hay in the middle of the school playground. "Allemande once into the night." There were strings of colored lights all around the jungle gym and monkey bars.

"First-the-left-hand-then-the-right-hand," Koo said under his breath. He and Jazz were square dancing with other children. The grownups were gathered in a circle around them, clapping their hands in time to the caller's words. Jazz saw Granny Hoe dishing out ice cream by the cake table. Grandpa Putter had gone across the playground to smoke a cigar.

"Change your partner, shuffle your feet," the caller cried.

"One-two-three, change partners, swing around," Koo muttered.

"You're making me lose the beat," Jazz whispered, skipping in rhythm over to the next boy.

Koo ignored her. He watched the other kids' feet.

"Give your new partner a tidy greet," the caller shouted out.

Koo figured he should bow, because the other boys did. "One-two-three, bow," he counted. His partner curtsied back.

"Dance in a circle hand in hand," the caller said.

Koo grabbed the hands of the girls on either side of him. He knew what to do! They danced around in a circle.

"Come back home and take a stand!" The caller was finished. Koo grinned and hopped to the side he'd started on. Finished.

Jazz was in the middle of the circle, looking confused.

Koo held out his hand to her. She took it. "I didn't know the steps," she said, trying to go back to their original places.

But Koo led her out of the circle. "You stay

here," he said, "until you get a new partner." He was eager to find someone who knew the steps.

"I will *not* stay here," Jazz said. "I'm staying with you."

"No," Koo answered.

The fiddler started another song. Mad at each other, Jazz and Koo walked over to the ice-cream table.

Koo watched the toe of Granny's boot. Tap-tap-tap-tap. Granny swung her skirt and clapped her hands in time to the music.

"Why don't you dance, Granny?" Koo asked her.

Granny shrugged. "I haven't danced in years," she said. "I don't know if I still know how."

Across the playground, Jazz saw Grandpa in his uniform. His boots twinkled when he tap-tap-tap-tapped along with the music. She took him a bowl of ice cream.

"Why don't you dance?" she asked him.

"I've always been too busy for this sort of thing," he said, spooning up some ice cream. "Or too old."

"Even Koo can dance," she told him.

"I don't have a partner," Grandpa replied.

"I know where you can find one," Jazz said. She held out her hand.

"Why, I'd love to dance with you," Grandpa said, putting down the bowl. But Jazz didn't take him to the middle of the playground. Instead, she walked them back to the ice-cream table.

"Oh no," Grandpa gasped. *"She* wouldn't want to dance with me."

"Come on," Jazz said, pulling him along.

Granny was still clapping her hands. Someone tapped her on the shoulder.

"Shall we give it a go?"

Koo looked up. It was the fireman who had helped them at the parade, asking Granny to dance.

"I'd be dee-lighted," Granny Hoe said. "What is your name, young man?"

"C. C. MacDonald, at your service," he said, bowing low and whisking Granny off.

"Where'd they go?" Jazz asked Koo, frowning.

He pointed to Granny Hoe, twirling herself

around Mr. MacDonald. The caller was shouting out moves.

Jazz peeked at Grandpa. He was staring down. It was one of the few times when his face was purple, but he wasn't mad.

"I am *not* a stupid old crow—or whatever she said this afternoon at the parade," he said to his boots.

"Peacock," Jazz corrected.

Grandpa was rubbing one boot on the back of his leg when someone tapped his shoulder. "May I have this dance?" she asked. Jazz recognized the firelady who had loaded up their bikes.

"Well, I'll be," Grandpa said.

"His name is Grandpa Putter," Koo said. "What's your name?"

"I am Missy Goldwater," she replied. "It's a funny name for a firefighter, I know."

"It's not funny," Grandpa Putter said. "And I would be honored—even though I'm a bit rusty." He stood up straight. His boots glinted as he strode away.

Koo felt brave. He turned to Jazz. "May I?" he asked her, holding out his arm.

"You may," Jazz said. They moved grandly into the center of the playground for another dance.

But Jazz thought Koo bowed too soon. And Koo knew Jazz curtsied too late. It was time to find other partners.

Counting Eggs

With their hands over their ears, Jazz and
Koo sat on the sofa in Grandpa Putter's den.

Grandpa and Granny Hoe were fighting
again.

They were in the front hallway, arguing.

Jazz and Koo could hear every word.

They felt better covering their ears.

"It is *my* day," Granny Hoe insisted. "The
shop is closed and I only have today free. Today! Jazz! Koo! Come here, my little sweets."

Jazz had once liked being called a little sweet.
Now she only pushed her face into the sofa
cushions.

"We're going *out!*" Grandpa Putter answered. "I've been busy with meetings all week long, and *today* they are going with *me*. Children! Ready or not, let's go!"

Koo had once loved the words "Ready or not!" Now he only pulled a pillow from the couch and wrapped it around his head.

The arguing didn't go away.

Jazz turned from the cushions.

Koo unwrapped his head.

"What should we do?" Jazz asked him. He shook his head.

"They usually sound funny," Jazz added.

Koo didn't answer.

"Why don't they stop this time?"

Koo was quiet.

"They sound like they mean business," Jazz told him. Koo was looking at his feet, matching one shoe to the other.

"Koo! Why aren't you helping?" Jazz cried.

"I'm scared," he told her.

"Me too," she said. "It's never been like this."

They were both quiet, listening.

"We need someone to settle it," Jazz finally said.

Counting Eggs

"Once and for all," Koo said.

"Like a sheriff," Jazz told him.

"No," said Koo, standing up. "We need a judge! A judge will make them like each other."

Jazz jumped off the couch. "The judge in the big green house by the traffic light. Old What's-his-name Grandpa calls him."

"That's what *Granny* calls him!" Koo shouted.

"See?" Jazz said. "They already agree."

They ran to the door and peeked down the hall.

"You've *always* been a blustering billy goat!" Granny Hoe was saying. "I'm not leaving without those children."

"Bully!" Grandpa blurted. "You think you can *bully* me!"

Jazz and Koo stayed out of sight, tiptoeing down the hall toward the kitchen, then out the garage door.

"We'll ride our bikes," Koo said. Grandpa had bought him a new front wheel. "No time for crack-ups. I'll give it my best shot."

"As long as we stop at corners," Jazz said.

The sound of the arguing faded as they rode down the driveway, across the brick road, around the cemetery, to the judge's house.

Jazz read the mailbox. "Judge Jefferson Atticus Polemos Shepherd. This is it," she told Koo. They left their bikes by the big yew tree and walked up the steps to the front door.

"It was my idea to come here," Koo said. "So you pull the rope." He pointed to a loop of gold cord. It was hanging from an eagle's beak near the knob. Jazz yanked it.

The door creaked, then swung open. Jazz and Koo stood there waiting for someone to say, "Come in." No one did. They stepped through the opening.

"H-hello!" Jazz called. A tall man in a silky, shiny purple robe appeared from behind the door. His red pants flapped around his ankles. On his head was a hat, deep red and shaped like an upside-down coffee can. It had a swinging tassel just like the doorbell's. He had a scarf over his eyes.

"Why is he blindfolded?" Koo whispered in Jazz's ear.

"Are you the judge?" asked Jazz.

"Who's there?" the man asked, grasping the

Counting Eggs

knot that held the blindfold to his eyes. "From the sound of your voice, I'd say you're short. I'll lean over." He did. "Help me get this unsnarled. I was just sorting out my spice rack. Throwing away the old ones. The nose knows what the eyes can't see," he said.

Jazz picked at the knot.

Koo heard a clucking noise—no, many clucking noises. Chickens!

The blindfold came off. The man stood up. "Aha! You are not short! You are children! And I am Judge—well, Judge What's-his-name. What can I do for you?" Jazz and Koo looked at each other.

"We need someone to help us," Jazz said.

"Our grandparents don't like each other," Koo added.

"I don't handle divorces," the judge said.

"But they aren't married," Koo protested.

"Problem solved," the judge said. "Now, would you like to meet the girls?" Koo looked around him.

"No, we wouldn't," Jazz told him. "Our grandparents argue."

"All the time," Koo said.

"What about?" the judge asked.

"About everything," Koo answered.

"Mostly about us," Jazz said. Koo wasn't being very helpful, she thought.

"What about your parents?" the judge said. "Can't they keep the old creakers under control?" They followed him down the hall toward the sound of the clucking. Koo noticed his slippers. The toes turned up and had little bells on them. He wanted a pair just like them.

"We're staying with our Grandpa Putter— and our Granny Hoe—while our parents are on a trip. Overseas," Jazz managed to say.

"In—abroad," Koo added, still staring at the shoes. "On business. They sell kids' apparel —jeans and shoes—but not like those," he said, pointing.

"So they're too far away to give you a hand with—hm," the judge said. "Well! Children! Come with me. First we gather some eggs. It always helps me think."

"I *did* hear chickens," Koo said.

"Well, that's true, my boy," the judge told him. "The girls do make noise. Sixty-six of 'em. This week. Good layers. They've been with me a long time—well, they're descendants now, of course, but I knew their ancestors." He stopped, took his funny hat off, and scratched his head, then put the hat on again. The tassel swayed like the pendulum of a grandfather clock.

"What I mean is," the judge continued, "that I've had a bunch of 'em at any one time. There."

The three of them went down a tile hallway. Jazz's and Koo's sneakers made no noise. The judge's slippers shuffled along in front of them. The hallway ended and they were in a greenhouse full of chickens, each sitting in a straw-filled nest on rows of shelves.

The judge walked up to one chicken, pushed her aside gently, and pulled an egg from the nest. He placed it in a mixing bowl that he had taken from a shelf by the door.

"But what about our problem?" Jazz said. "Do they have to go to court?"

"Looks as if it's a *tennis* court they need," he said. "I know your grandmother," he said. "Can't believe she's the bickering kind."

"She is when she's with Grandpa," Jazz said.

"We know about divorce," Koo said. "But does Grandpa Putter have to pay ali-alimony?"

Jazz didn't know whether Koo was being stupid or *she* was.

"If they're not married, they're not divorced," said the judge. *"Ipso facto*, no alimony."

"Is there any other *ipso facto* we can use with Grandpa?" Jazz asked. Koo thought Jazz was being silly.

"I know your grandfather," the judge said. "Can't believe he's the bickering kind either."

"He is when he's with Granny Hoe," Jazz said again.

"Then, seems to me you should keep them apart. Or you two should stay away from them."

"But we want to be with both of them," Jazz told him.

"And we don't want them to fight," said Koo.

"Who wins the fights?" the judge asked.

Jazz and Koo looked at each other.

"Both of them?" Koo suggested.

"Neither of them?" Jazz asked.

"Pretty equal match?" the judge asked. Jazz and Koo nodded. "Sounds like fair play to me," he said. "No need to worry." They followed him again down the hall. He led them to the kitchen. "I may be a spice expert, and I may know twenty-two different ways to make an omelet," he said, "but I can't say I can unscramble *your* problem." He opened the door to the large refrigerator. It was filled with eggs. No milk. No cheese. No soda pop.

Eggs in the door.

Eggs in bags.

Eggs in boxes.

Eggs in baskets.

Eggs in bottles.

The judge looked at the mixing bowl full of eggs in his arms. "Timing is everything," he told them. "Looks like these eggs belong to you." He handed them to Jazz.

"But maybe they'll get sick," Jazz protested.

The judge looked puzzled. "The eggs?"

"Grandpa and Granny," Koo added, thinking that Jazz wasn't as good at explaining things as she used to be. "Grandpa turns purple, and his buttons pop. Granny gets noisy and keeps saying 'Bah!' a lot when they argue."

"Noise?" the judge said. "Lots of good things are noisy. Fireworks booming, chickens

clucking, thunderstorms crashing. And, God knows, lawyers are noisy—*and* kids. Now you had better get those eggs home and make sure they stay cold. Don't want them to hatch."

At the front hallway, the judge picked up his blindfold. Outside, there were sirens. He opened the door.

"Now, that's one loud noise I never like," he said, watching as a speeding police car streamed past his house.

"Jazz, it's headed toward Grandpa Putter's!" Koo said. He ran toward his bike.

"Thanks for everything, Judge, but we have to go," Jazz said as she put the eggs carefully in her bicycle basket and gave him back the bowl.

"I can drive you in the old Lincoln," he called.

"Thanks, but we can't wait," said Jazz. She hopped on her bike and rode toward the traffic light.

"You can stop by for eggs anytime," he yelled, waving at them with his blindfold.

"I'm scared," Koo said as they pedaled up the shortcut through the cemetery.

"Do you think they—you know—slugged each other?" Jazz asked.

Koo was silent. "I think that's supposed to be only on TV," he finally said. "But you never know."

Two cars, one of them a police car, were in Grandpa's driveway next to Granny Hoe's truck. Jazz and Koo no sooner rode up than both Grandpa and Granny burst out of the house. Granny was in Grandpa's arms, crying. He was patting her back. Rosalind and Ben were right behind them.

"Uh-oh," Koo said.

"Uh-oh," Jazz said.

"You scamps!" Grandpa Putter cried. "Where were you?"

"Children! You scared us very nearly into early graves," Granny shrieked.

"Maybe we made them like each other, after all," Jazz whispered to Koo.

"We didn't think just *going* to the judge would do it," Koo replied.

Jazz and Koo noticed that no one seemed to want any answers. They were surrounded by happy older people and staring police officers.

"Looks as if we can close the book on this kidnapping," a policeman said.

"We went to Judge—hm," Koo told Granny. "He gave us eggs."

"Hundreds of eggs," Jazz said.

"And we can get more every day," Koo added.

"Free," Jazz said.

"For your soup kitchen," Grandpa Putter said to Granny Hoe, hugging Jazz to his side.

"No no," Granny said, with her hands on Koo's shoulders. "For the Buffalo Fund bake sale at your church," she told Grandpa.

"I insist," Grandpa Putter said. "Don't you need them for your new project on the Reservation?"

"The Buffalo Fund wildlife aims need support, too," Granny answered. "They'll need hundreds of eggs for those cakes."

Jazz and Koo waved to the police car as it drove away.

"But Ben told me that the Native Americans could raise free-range chickens to sell to the Waterworks and other restaurants," Grandpa said, his smile stiff and his voice getting louder.

"And Rosalind told me that she had never seen more excitement than that for the Buffalo Fund's accomplishments," Granny replied sweetly but firmly.

"Granny," Koo said.

"Grandpa," Jazz said.

The grandparents looked at the children.

"What?" Grandpa Putter said.

"What is it?" Granny Hoe said.

"You can both have eggs," Jazz told them.

"There are enough for everyone, the judge said," Koo added.

For a minute they were silent as they walked back toward Grandpa's house. Then Granny spoke.

"Okay," she said.

"Both," said Grandpa Putter. "Never thought of it that way."

"*Both!*" Jazz and Koo chorused.

Gathering

"Sparklers?" Koo called out.

"Check," Jazz answered. She was packing everything into a picnic basket.

"Marshmallows?" Koo asked.

"Check," Jazz told him.

"Chocolate bars?" Koo said.

"Check. And graham crackers," Jazz replied.

"I didn't *ask* for graham crackers," Koo protested. "You have to wait for me to ask."

"Okay, okay," Jazz said. She pulled the graham crackers out of the picnic basket.

"Ready?" Koo asked.

"Ready," Jazz answered.

"Graham crackers?" Koo asked.

"I just *told* you that we have graham crackers," Jazz said, standing up.

"Then say, 'Check,' " Koo told her.

"But you know that we have them," Jazz told him.

"Say 'Check!' " Koo demanded. "We decided. Grandpa says it's good to use lists. That's why he gave us this one. So just say 'Check.' "

"*Check!*" Jazz shouted. She threw the graham crackers on the floor and stamped off. "Check, check, check, *check*, CHECK!" she yelled from the next room.

Koo waited. He put down his list. By now he could read even the long words on it.

He looked at the chocolate bars. His hands were about to reach toward them. He put his hands in his pockets.

He waited some more. Then he called, "Are you coming back?"

Jazz didn't answer.

"If you don't come help me, I'll never speak to you again," Koo called. He looked at the chocolate bars once more. Granny Hoe always said that she could attract more bees with honey than with vinegar. He didn't know why she would want to have bees around, but he knew that she meant it was better not to be grouchy.

"I think we have too many chocolate bars," he called out. "Maybe we should each have one now."

Jazz still didn't answer.

"What I mean is that there is one extra chocolate bar and I think you should have it," he called. "That's what I really think."

Jazz stood at the doorway. She, too, had her hands in her pockets. "One extra?" she asked. "Not two?"

Koo looked at the list. He shook his head.

Jazz walked over to him and looked at the list. She looked at the chocolate bars. "What I really think," she said, "is that if we didn't have that stupid list, we could have as many chocolate bars as we want right now."

"Probably one each?" Koo asked.

Jazz leaned over the picnic basket. "Probably two each," she said. "What do you think?"

Koo picked up the list. "Get rid of this list?" he said.

She nodded.

"Check," he said, and ripped it down the middle.

"Check," Jazz repeated, and tossed Koo a chocolate bar.

"I thought we were supposed to have more chocolate bars than this," Granny Hoe said later that day, peeking into the picnic basket.

"Did you children pack everything on the list?" Grandpa Putter asked. He was trudging toward the park between Jazz and Koo.

"Yes," said Koo.

"No," said Jazz.

"No," said Koo. He was afraid Grandpa would turn purple.

"Yes," said Jazz. She was afraid she would turn blue from laughing.

"I'm sure we have enough of everything," Granny Hoe said.

"Be prepared," Grandpa grumbled. "How could they not follow a simple list?"

"We did follow a list," Jazz said, "while we were packing."

"But you didn't buy enough supplies," Koo said, "for us to pack."

"I didn't?" Grandpa asked, scratching under

his hatband. "Oh well, I'm sorry about that. I didn't mean to blame you, Koo."

Granny peered closely at Koo's face. "I think you're too quick with your apologies, Mr. Putter. This boy has chocolate on his chin." She stood up straight again. "But this is the first time I've ever heard you admit you might occasionally be wrong."

Grandpa just harrumphed once.

They were all together. The sky was navy blue by the time they spread out Grandpa's old army blanket on the long green grass in the park.

The Fourth of July bonfire pile was so big it could reach to the sky. It was taller than Grandpa Putter or Granny Hoe.

A pile of bits and scraps and fractured objects pointed upward.

Higher than the clock tower of City Hall.

Higher than the church bell.

People had said that the smoke from the fire could be seen all the way to the Twin Cities International Airport.

Old chairs with three legs. Fence poles chopped to pieces. Tables with broken tops. Paper lampshades without lamps. Kitchen cupboards without doors. Broomsticks too short to sweep with. Bureaus without drawers, and drawers without bureaus. A large wardrobe missing its back and scraps of lumber too small to be useful. The firefighters would light the entire pile as soon as it was dark.

Jazz was chilly with excitement. A bonfire tonight, and tomorrow, who knew? Grandpa and Granny said that their parents would be back any day. Any day. *Any day.*

Koo was worried that the pile was too large this year. If the whole town caught on fire, and if everyone had to move to a new town, how would their parents find them when they came back from their trip?

"What a waste," Granny said, pointing to an old chair. "We ought to be making a fourth leg to match that chair's other three. It could be useful again." She unloaded the picnic basket onto the blanket.

"Nonsense," Grandpa Putter said. "It's the one time of the year when it's good to toss out the old and bring in the new." Koo sat in Grandpa's lap.

"And sometimes what's old is plenty good,"

Gathering

Granny Hoe answered, while Jazz leaned on her. "Like your blanket here."

Grandpa looked at the blanket. "It's seen some fire," he said. "It has served me well."

"Look, it's the firelady," Jazz said. "She doesn't have her uniform on." Miss Goldwater waved at them as she roped off the area around the pile of junk.

"What *are* those ropes for?" Jazz protested. Koo stood up.

"Why don't you ask Miss Goldfish?" Granny Hoe said.

"Goldwater," Grandpa Putter said.

"Coldwater?" asked Jazz. Granny and Jazz both giggled, but Granny quickly stopped.

"*Gold*water," Koo insisted.

Granny giggled once again.

"That's a fine way to teach children some manners," Grandpa said in his stern voice. "You might as well skip and scream and chew bubble gum like them."

"Don't you tell *me* what to teach them and what not," Granny said. "I tell them what's fitting and it's up to them to figure things out for themselves." Granny pulled her arm away from Jazz and stood up. "And you're *not* going to have your way with these children even if you're the next best thing to drumsticks and Father Christmas."

Grandpa held his sides and chuckled.

"I'm going to see Miss Goldwater," Jazz said.

Koo remembered how nice the firelady had been about his bent-up bike. "I'll come with you," he said to Jazz, not wanting to be left out.

"Hello, you two," Miss Goldwater said as they approached. "What's up?"

"Why do you have ropes?" Jazz asked.

"So that people won't get hurt by the fire," Miss Goldwater replied.

"I don't like the bonfire," Koo said.

"Yes, you do," Jazz told him. "Every year you love it."

"This year I don't," Koo said. He hadn't told Jazz that he was worried.

"But without fire, you'd eat raw hot dogs," Miss Goldwater said.

"I think you can die from eating uncooked hot dogs," Jazz said. "I think I learned that at school."

Gathering

"And marshmallows," Koo added. "They have to be cooked. For graham cracker and chocolate bar sandwiches. Cold marshmallows won't melt the chocolate so they're—you know—gooey."

"Well, we can't have anyone dying from raw hot dogs or cold marshmallows," the firelady said. "I'll show you where you can cook."

Koo ran back to grab their things. Grandpa Putter and Granny Hoe were sitting on opposite sides of the blanket, not speaking.

Jazz and Koo had their plates full of cooked hot dogs as they walked toward the blanket. Now Grandpa Putter and Granny Hoe were sitting very close together, staring up at the sky. As they walked nearer, they heard Grandpa Putter say, "Just for tonight, let's not fight."

"I don't want to fight," Granny replied, "not tonight. Not with the bonfire, and the fireworks—and have you ever seen so many stars?"

"No, Jean, I haven't," Grandpa told her.

"It's just beautiful, Eugene," Granny Hoe answered.

Jazz looked at Koo. "What's going on?" she whispered.

"I don't know," Koo said.

"You can call me Gene, you know," Grandpa Putter said. He saw Jazz and Koo with a pile of hot dogs. "Offer one to your grandmother first," he said. "Here's some pickles and relish."

Granny Hoe's face lit up with a smile. "I don't usually have pickles on my hot dogs," she said. "But since you offered, why yes."

Jazz and Koo almost didn't recognize the tall man who strolled past them—he was in plaid shorts and a polka-dot shirt instead of silky pajamas. But they knew his voice.

"Me oh my," Judge Jefferson Atticus Polemos Shepherd said. "I'm so disappointed," he told the children. "I was expecting real fireworks."

They thought he was talking about the bonfire, but he was staring right at Grandpa Putter and Granny Hoe.

Granny Hoe stopped halfway into her first bite of hot dog and said, "Hello, Judge . . . Judge . . . well, Judge. Nice to see you."

Grandpa Putter finished spreading a napkin

delicately on Granny Hoe's lap. He looked up. "Hello, Judge. Fine night."

"Nope," the judge replied. "Fizzle, sizzle, phftt. No sparks anywhere." He walked off, shaking his head.

Mr. MacDonald and Miss Goldwater walked around the bonfire, lighting it on all sides. It started to crackle in the front.

The flames climbed and curled like vines of ivy.

Soon Jazz and Koo could no longer see any tables or chairs or colors or fences. There was only the white fire in the inky sky.

Boom! Boom! Overhead, fireworks rushed through the black night. Smoke poured into the sky. Koo felt the fireworks drumming in his chest. Jazz chewed on her hot dog. People crowded around the fire. They looked like shadows with marshmallow faces.

A man and a woman broke away from the shadows and came toward them. They seemed to walk right out of the fire.

"It's Ben and Rosalind!" said Koo.

"No, it's Mr. MacDonald and Miss Cold— Goldwater!" Jazz said.

The two people were looking around. They

spoke to the judge, who pointed toward Jazz and Koo and Grandpa Putter and Granny Hoe.

It was dark as charcoal away from the fire. It was hard for the children to see anything.

"Goldwater is a lovely woman," Jazz and Koo heard Grandpa Putter say. "And what a dancer!"

"You and that young girl!" Granny Hoe said, moving away from Grandpa on the blanket.

"She has been to the White House, you know," said Grandpa. "She's seen Lincoln's ghost—right there in front of his bedroom."

"Bah! *Bunk!*"

"What about you and that boy with the long hair and show-biz bow tie?" Grandpa said, standing up abruptly.

"What do you mean by that, you vain old bat?" Granny Hoe cried, standing up next to him. "MacDonald, too, had *his* glory. His speech on the steps of Capitol Hill was written up in all the papers."

"*Poppycock!*" Grandpa said.

Koo and Jazz were still staring at the couple coming toward them.

"Any day!" Jazz said. She started waving. "Over here, over here!" she screamed.

"Over here!" Koo cried, putting his hot dog down. Now he loved the bonfire. It could burn forever. He wasn't worried anymore.

Jazz and Koo stood up.

Grandpa Putter and Granny Hoe were still saying terrible things to each other, but Jazz and Koo could barely hear them, not over the popping and the crackling of the bonfire.

And then they ran. Jazz and Koo ran straight for their parents' arms. They were back. And Just in Time.